AF581114

KAUAI ROOSTER *Stories*

{ And Other Tropical Tales }

ROGER LEPLEY

Book Cover by Wes Garman and KUHN Design Group

Book Design by KUHN Design Group and Roger Lepley

Edited by Thomas Thinnes

Illustrations/photos by:
Kimberly Barber
Kristy Lepley
Adobe Stock
"Chicken Divan" painting by Fanny Bilodeau

ISBN 979-8-218-31318

There was a Kaua'i rooster named Red
Who let crowing go to his head.
The noise that he made,
Shrill for what he weighed,
Shook the tourists from their beds!

To Ellie, Gavin, Andrew & Evan

Contents

Introduction: Why all the crowing on Kaua'i, Hawaii 13

1. Local Deputy Interviews Kaua'i Rooster 17
2. Early Morning Rooster Ruckus Ends with Seminar in Kapa'a 21
3. Kaua'i Roosters Demand Royalties From Local Artist 27
4. Kaua'i Roosters Flying in Formation? 31
5. Kaua'i's Roosters Alarmed at Island's Rising Human Population 35
6. Rooster Regiment 39
7. Why Did the Chicken Cross Halfway? 45
8. Kaua'i Roosters Gain Altitude and Attitude 49
9. Roosters Spotted Using Missing Laptops on Kaua'i 53
10. Early-Morning Crime Results in Luncheon at Kentucky Fried Chicken 57
11. Rare 'Tofu Bird' Sighted Near Kaua'i's Haena State Park 61
12. Kaua'i Roosters Rate Sports Illustrated Swimsuit Issue 65
13. The World's Oldest Baby Chick or Is This a Stink about Nothing? 71
14. Kaua'i Rooster on a Binge? 75

15. Kaua'i Roosters and One Wild Turkey on Thanksgiving 79

16. Rooster Asks, "Why the Masks?" 83

17. Unusual Early Gathering Sited at Anini Beach 89

18. Kaua'i Reporter Interviews Volcano Goddess Pele 93

19. Too-Early Morning Joe 97

20. De-Roostering Our Island? Well, Not That Way! 101

21. Chicken Divan 105

The Author 111

Introduction

Why all the crowing on Kaua'i, Hawaii

"Why are there so many chickens on Kaua'i?" is a common question from visitors to this lush island.

To be certain, there are thousands of roosters, hens and baby chicks roaming underfoot on Kaua'i. If you live on Kaua'i you've probably almost tripped over one and said some interesting things. The recent estimate places 450,000 wild "jungle fowl" on this 550-square-mile island, the fourth largest in the Hawaiian chain.

The current human population is about 75,000. So, six chickens per person. It is estimated—by those who make up estimates—that there are equal numbers of hens to roosters, but you might come to your own conclusions if you're trying to sleep past 5:00 a.m. on Kaua'i. The chicken population differs in many ways from the human population, of course, but one of the most obvious is that the guys seem to talk more than the gals. And more in the morning. And louder.

The common theory on why there are so many free-roaming chickens is due to the hurricanes of 1982 and 1992. The destructive storms blasted chicken pens open and the domestic flock burgeoned out to become what is now the massive conglomerate of colorful jungle birds.

Also, only about 10 percent of the island is inhabited by humans, which leaves plenty of lush territory for fowl cohabitation. And, except for rapidly traveling Ford F150 pickup trucks, there are no natural predators such as mongoose on the island. For more information on the chicken population, plenty can be found on the internet. Or you can go to Kaua'i to observe and count on your own. Make up your own statistics, as I sometimes do.

If you'd like further information about the unusual and very talented Deputy Robert Moakane, the "Rooster Whisperer," whom you will meet in some stories, you'll just have to read the stories in this book again and hope to learn more. I have re-read the stories and *not* learned more, however. The internet will refer you to my stories, by the way.

Local Deputy Interviews Kaua'i Rooster

Last week, Deputy Robert Moakane, the renowned "Rooster Whisperer" of Kaua'i had the opportunity to interview one of the island's older, more experienced and apparently quite "well read" roosters. The deputy described the interview, which took place just outside the Shave Ice in Hanalei, as a bizarre encounter, but something that he'd been long thinking about attempting with a rooster. He came across one that seemed very bright and surprisingly articulate. The "whisperer" part of it, he explains, is his uncanny ability to understand what roosters are thinking. This is a transcript of a recording he made of the "conversation." Of course, he had to repeat out loud everything that the rooster was thinking so that it could be recorded. The following has been edited for brevity.

"Hi, Mr. Rooster, I'm Robert. I'm going to repeat everything that I think you're saying into this microphone."

"Cool. Call me Red."

"How are you, Red?"

"I'm fine."

"What does 'I'm fine' mean, you know, to a rooster?"

"I have six wives and I haven't a clue where any of them are."

"So, you're fine."

"That's what I thought."

"What do you mean 'that's what you thought'? Isn't that's what you said?"

"No, that's what I thought. You're the one who's actually saying something out loud, remember? I'm just strutting around here thinking while you figure out what I'm thinking."

"Oh, yes, sorry."

"OK, but could you hurry? I haven't eaten for, like, 10 minutes."

"OK, so how does a rooster learn the English language?"

"I read stuff."

"Like what kind of stuff?"

"Litter."

"You read litter?"

"Do you want me to repeat *everything* so you don't have to?"

"No, I just can't get used to the fact that I'm communicating with a rooster."

"You're not very good at it."

"Sorry, but I don't know anyone else who can talk to roosters."

"Actually, I got to hand it to you. You're the first big dude I've ever thought with."

"'Dude', that's an interesting word. Where did you learn that?"

"I've been pecking around the lanai at the Quiksilver store. Dudes, dudes, dudes. Hang 10, hang loose, hang over. Ya listen, ya learn stuff."

"So you've learned language by listening to people talk and by reading litter? Amazing."

"Sometimes you feel like a nut, sometimes you don't. Melts in your mouth not in your hand. Longboard Beer, The Breakfast of Champions, I'm lovin' it. By the way, what's fructose corn syrup? You know what? I'm surprised bugs aren't smarter; they're crawling all over the litter but they don't stop and read any of it. I love bugs. They're so cute. And delicious."

"You eat a lot of bugs, do you?"

"Yeah, well, depends where I'm pecking. If I wander off to Kalypso Cafe, the big folks toss me fries and burger buns. I like the fries better but they give me gas."

"Yeah, me too. How about that? We have something in common!"

"Cool. Next time I see you at Kalypso, I'm not stoppin' to say hi if you know what I mean. So, I'm gonna trot off to the jungle now and check out a new family of centipedes I heard about."

"OK, and I need to get to Foodland and pick up some lunch, maybe one of those rotisserie chick...oh, ahh...well, some fresh veggies."

"Right. Don't eat anybody I know. See ya."

"Been fun. See ya, Dude."

Early Morning Rooster Ruckus Ends with Seminar in Kapa'a

Fourteen unruly roosters on Kaua'i were brought in for questioning by Deputy Robert Moakane after several north shore residents and visitors complained of excessive crowing in the morning.

Comments such as, "We all know the roosters get up before we do, but this was just plain ridiculous," and, "It sounded like an Italian soccer game, by golly," were heard. One eyewitness reported, "We'd been told that Deputy Moakane has a way with roosters and can get them to quiet down, so we specifically asked for him to come. It was that bad."

The deputy took the roosters away for what he called "a seminar," and returned them later in the day to the original location.

This reporter learned that the deputy has spent his entire life in the

Hawaiian Islands and is not only fluent with the Hawaiian language but also claims to be conversant with a few of the islands' roosters. "Sort of a 'horse-whisperer' kind of thing," said the deputy, "but with roosters instead of horses. Having lived here forever, I just acquired a sixth sense about what they are thinking. Some of the conversations are pretty interesting, especially later in the day when they are done scurrying around waking everybody up."

When asked whether he actually whispers to the roosters, he stated, "It's not so much whispering, because I'd swear they don't hear worth a hoot, so I've taken to either shouting until they stop to pay attention or I just stare at the them until they wonder what I'm up to. That's how I managed to get them into the van for our little session this morning."

One eyewitness reported that Deputy Moakane backed his police van to the scene and stared the roosters down until they all reluctantly walked up the little plank and into the back. "The roosters looked a bit embarrassed and timid as we watched them slowly climb the ramp," said a visitor from Pentwater, Mich. "They didn't look around much and sort of had their heads down. I don't know what he said but apparently the deputy had conveyed that he was pretty disappointed in their behavior, I'd guess."

The seminar that the deputy mentioned was more of a tour that he gave the island fowl. Apparently, this is not the first time that he's done this and he believes that it's effective for a few months or so. "Gets them to think twice about creating a major ruckus like the one this morning," Moakane says. "We don't mind so much if they crow in the early morning because, after all, they are roosters and that's what roosters do. But they were just out of hand and thoroughly obnoxious today."

This reporter asked Deputy Mokane to describe the seminar. "Well, I'd heard that the Lion's Club was having a fund-raising BBQ in Kapa'a at noon so it was pretty easy. The van has plenty of windows so when we got to where the guys were basting the chickens on that huge, smoking BBQ grill, I told the roosters to get on the top of the seatbacks and check out the scenery. Whoa, I tell you it never fails! Those birds got quiet, real quick. I only had to stay there about 30 seconds and they were poking each other and pointing, as best they could, all wide-eyed and sort of shaking. I slowly turned the van around and headed back up north. That ride was the quietest one I'd had in quite a while."

Kaua'i Roosters Demand Royalties From Local Artist

Six ostensibly determined jungle roosters have been paying special attention to the home of Kapa'a artist Fanny Bilodeau, according to her husband Ron Bilodeau. "I believe these birds have been intent on telling us something, but I really think they're trying to talk specifically to Fanny," said Ron when this reporter visited their home to learn more.

"She's the one who's known to paint Kaua'i's roosters in both real and absurd situations," he said. "So Fanny asked me to investigate the hullabaloo outside her studio. It's as though they actually know what some of her paintings portray and they seem to want to talk with her. Although, that sounds nuts, doesn't it?"

To determine what may be sparking the rooster commotion, this reporter researched further and was reminded that some of Fanny's artwork features the birds performing amazing and unbelievable feats. I first admired her art a few years ago while munching on banana macadamia-nut pancakes at Kountry Kitchen in Kapa'a. For example, Fanny's art includes one piece with a rooster flying an open-cockpit airplane, another surfing and so on.

Knowing that Kaua'i Deputy Robert Moakane may be of some help with deciphering the mystery, I asked him to meet with me, along with the Bilodeaus and the roosters. The deputy is known to be a "Rooster Whisperer" and to actually be able to communicate in some way with the jungle fowl. This reporter has documented his unusual talents in a few stories in *The Garden Island* newspaper in which Deputy Moakane employed his special skills to assist with rooster-related dilemmas.

The meeting was set for mid-morning after the roosters had finished their well-known "wake-up" services for the island. The ten of us gathered in the Bilodeau yard around an outside table. Four of us were in lawn chairs while others pecked on the ground nearby.

As soon as the deputy arrived, the roosters took notice and glanced at each other. Then they slowly backed away as if to say, "Uh-oh, what'd we do now?!"

The deputy immediately put them at ease, crouching down to their level and offering a handful of chicken feed while staring intently into their eyes. The roosters lifted and cocked their heads a bit, then began chattering or chirping or some such noise directly at the deputy.

He nodded knowingly, got up from his crouch and pulled up a chair to address Fanny. "I'm pretty sure that the roosters are looking for some type of, what I might call, "royalty payments", from you. You know, for your using their images in your paintings," he said in a noticeably serious tone but smiling at the same time, obviously attempting not to laugh and put the roosters off, because the six appeared glued to his every action and statement.

"Really?! Oh, well, I guess I can understand that," Fanny said in a thoughtful way that seemed to reflect on the odd-but-interesting information she had just received. "Well, then," she said talking directly to the roosters. "How can I do that?"

Ron looked at her as though she were nuts. The roosters looked at her as though to convey appreciation for her understanding. They approached her slowly and maybe, I might add, even affectionately.

"Well, I'm not sure what to suggest," said Deputy Moakane. "Perhaps it would be appropriate to offer them what they value most, which is food and respect. I'd say you set out a bit of grain each day, away from the house, and see if that does the job. Of course, feeding the wild jungle fowl is, shall we say, frowned upon, but I believe it will be OK under the circumstances."

"So what you're saying," asked Ron "is that some of Fanny's models for her paintings would be happy working for 'chicken feed'?"

"Yep, that's about it! It may not seem like much to you or me, but for them, chicken feed is perfect!"

The roosters nodded in apparent triumph, bowed to the deputy, then to Fanny, looked each of us in the eye and strutted off with their combs held high.

Kaua'i Roosters Flying in Formation?

Seven island roosters were seen flying over Kaua'i's Anini Beach in the morning in "Blue Angels-style formation," according to island resident Tootsie Yeager of Kilauea.

"It was startling," she says. "My husband Chuck and I were walking the beach early and, without any warning, these seven huge birds dove down right over us in perfect formation. Then the two birds on the ends peeled off on their own. The other five flew straight up and then straight down, and the other two came back to each end. They joined the five, swooped back up into a perfect 'V' and headed for Kilauea Lighthouse, where we think they landed. Chuck took plenty of pictures with his iPhone and it wasn't until he downloaded them that we realized they were all roosters. I didn't know roosters could even fly, let alone do air-show stunts!"

As it turns out, there is considerably more to the story. After hearing the Yeager's account, this reporter headed over to the lighthouse, knowing that it was also the Kilauea Point National Wildlife Refuge and the home to many tropical birds. I was curious what the staff might know about whether roosters could actually fly distances and had they seen the seven in flight.

"Well, we didn't think roosters could fly very far, but, yes, we saw the birds in question," said volunteer Dixie Whistler. "We noticed them for the first time about six days ago, up on the bluff just to the south where many albatross land and nest. We hadn't said anything to anyone as we didn't have enough facts, but, as unbelievable as it sounds, it appears that the albatross were giving the seven roosters flight lessons.

"At first," she said, "we thought that the two species were simply becoming quite friendly, which is unusual, but they seemed to be meeting and, if you'll believe this, communicating in some way. Heads were bobbing and wings pointing and so forth. Using our best binoculars, we all watched at various times trying to decipher what was actually happening."

"If you've ever seen an albatross take off or land, you'd wonder why the roosters chose them as their flight instructors," said volunteer Liz Tinney. "They don't call them gooney birds for nothing!"

"That's for sure," added Whistler. "An albatross is so fun to watch take off and then land. They often are very clumsy with their swaying and running takeoff, and then they sometimes bump their heads and flop around when landing. Their bodies are so big, it's kind of like watching a boxcar trying to land. But, when they're in the air, they are a wonder to behold as they soar gracefully with the wind."

"You know, maybe that's why the roosters are working with them," said Tinney. "Roosters also have huge bodies but are known to be able to generally only fly a few feet, maybe up to a low tree branch at best."

"I saw those seven come in yesterday morning as a group," said Refuge staff member Koa Wood. "Maybe the same time that the Yeagers saw them. It was rough. The roosters all flew to the bluff at the same time, which is something albatross don't do, and they tried to land all at once. The birds ended up in a tumbling mess with wings and legs flopping all over, feathers flying and lots of crowing as if they were swearing at each other. They didn't get up for quite a while and when they did they were limping and shaking their heads as if to say, 'That's the last time I'll do THAT!' They haven't been back today."

Coincidentally,—and no doubt unrelated but certainly interesting—this reporter noticed seven ruffled and limping roosters this morning on the lanai at Titus Kinimaka's Surfing School in Hanalei. They appeared to be checking out the surfboards.

Kaua'i's Roosters Alarmed at Island's Rising Human Population

Kaua'i's noted "Rooster Whisperer," Deputy Robert Moakane, has disclosed some surprising news concerning the island's chicken community.

If you're not familiar with Deputy Moakane, he's been touted locally as someone who may actually understand and perhaps even communicate with the island's fowl, much like documented horse whisperers.

"I don't pretend to have any supernatural powers," states Moakane." "It's just that the chickens and I seem to second-guess each other and we've had some interesting encounters."

According to the deputy, the wild chickens are concerned and even agitated about the growing human population on Kaua'i. "The roosters in particular are more vocal about it," he reports, "especially at dawn. I believe they are complaining that humans are practically everywhere. One rooster pecking around Ono-Char Burger seemed quite upset that so many humans were wandering all over the place while he was trying to eat.

"From what I can tell, they have set up chicken committees around the island to discuss the matter," says Moakane. "They apparently have looked at 1992's Hurricane Iniki as their personal 'Big Bang' event when they began assuming they were meant by some form of providence 'to take over' from a minority to a majority position and begin, eventually, to rule the island in some sort of "regal fowl manner."

"I know it sounds preposterous," said the deputy, "but just look at what's happened in the past 30 years. The chickens have accomplished quite a bit and have somehow even legally protected themselves in certain areas. I'm fairly sure they believe they've somehow influenced local ordinances through their support of various politicians sympathetic to the birds' well-being. Since I work for the public, it would be inappropriate for me to say that we've had a few 'bird-brained' politicians, but the thought is interesting. Don't quote me on that."

In any case, Moakane suggests that humans may want to reflect on what might be occurring. Besides the fact that the chicken population has grown undeterred, it also appears to be no mere coincidence that there are increasing numbers of artwork, signs, T-shirts, souvenirs and products,—such as coffee and cigars with rooster photos and likenesses—appearing on Kaua'i.

One rooster complained that he was taking his wife and young chicks up the Sleeping Giant Trail and was forced to gather them off into the forest several times to avoid being trampled by human hikers jogging up and down the trails. "To make matters even less pleasant, one of them was toting a white KFC take-out bag," the bird communicated to the deputy and added, "that's just insulting! It was all I could do to keep my babies from seeing that."

The deputy believes that the roosters are mostly concerned that humans have an unfair advantage. That is, the fowl have to increase population solely by breeding while the Kauaian human population is growing quickly by people flying from long distances to the island and eventually moving here. "The point is, and this seems somewhat ironic if you think about the fact that these are birds, the roosters are dismayed that humans can fly long distances and the birds can't!"

Rooster Regiment

OK, troops, listen up. The sun's peekin' up! Big morning!"

"But Captain Red, every mornin' is a big mornin'. Can't we sleep in just once? We're always workin' before the sun gets up!"

"Sleep in! Sleep in?! Reggie, are you crazy? These people depend on us! Trust me, they love our early-mornin' wake-up calls.! Especially the tourists. They're crazy about Kaua'i. It's paradise and they're not into sleepin' it away. They don't stay up late and party. They come here to rise at the crack of dawn and hit the beach. It's not a coincidence that breakfast, beach and bikini all start with 'B'."

"Captain, I really don't think the tourists like the crowin'. Two days ago, a guy in 24A came out with a broom lookin' for me. I know he was!"

"All part of the job."

"Yes, but he was swingin' that thing and swearin' and tellin' me to shut up! I almost had to fly to get away. I hardly ever fly. Scares me. And there's been worse than that. I heard that Ronnie, down in Hanalei, was taken into custody for interrogation and they may be grillin' him today."

"Yeah, I know, there're a few lazy visitors that don't understand Kaua'i. But, we can't let those slackers get in the way of us doin' our mornin' jobs. Remember Reggie, and this is important, the reason there are so many of us chickens here is no mystery. We're here to eventually dominate the island. Take it over. And until the time is right, we just need to do what comes natural."

"Gettin' up early and yellin' doesn't come natural to me."

"You're one strange bird. You know, your family has been at this for generations and hardly any of them have been injured or eaten."

"Yes, but...."

"Well, then maybe I should talk to the General and have you transferred."

"Transferred? Where? To do what?"

"It's more dangerous, but I know it's excitin'. Well, sort of."

"Oh, you don't mean the 'crossin'-the-road thing'?"

"Yes, I do. We need to keep that tradition up. How would it look if the big folks never saw us do that? I'll bet they talk about that a million times a day. Besides, what else is there?"

"I could do the other thing. You know, the one that's, well, the most fun. Sort of like moonlightin'? You know, helping to get more troops, so to speak?

"You mean girl friends? What do you know about that? You're barely four months old and, besides, that's more for the officers, not the new recruits. Let's talk about the road thing. You do that for a while, then we'll see about other duties."

"But, Captain, the crossin'-the-road thing, well….I…"

"You what? Oh, I know. You can say it. It's OK, go ahead."

"I'm chicken."

Why Did the Chicken Cross Halfway?

We've all heard the question. Especially on Kaua'i. Why did the chicken cross... well, you know the rest.

Here's the thing. Not long ago, a Kaua'i chicken went only halfway across the road,—Kuhio Highway to be specific—near *The Garden Island* newspaper offices, and stopped. For lunch. Perilous, eh? Furthermore, against all parental-safety advice, she brought her kids along.

"Hey kids, here's a great spot! Nice breeze, lots to see. Let's peck away at this slice of bread, then mosey on over to the parking lot at Kentucky Fried Chicken. Oh, wait, maybe not KFC..."

To put this impending-disaster story into a positive mode, I must tell you that it all ends well, but here's the rest of the story. I contacted Deputy Robert Moakane, the island's noted "Rooster Whisperer" who has an uncanny rapport with some unique roosters, and we arranged to meet near the spot. We hoped to find the fowl family for a chat. Deputy Moakane was intrigued and here's a recap of the "conversation" with the hen's mate and the chicks' dad:

"Hi Mister Rooster, can we chat?"

"Sure, what's on my mind?"

"Ha, got it. I think we've met before. I'm Deputy Moakane."

"Yes, I know. My name's Red, and yes you interviewed me a while ago. And now you want to talk about why one of my wives took some of my little kids halfway across the street, don't you? I wasn't pleased."

"So, yes, that's the topic. What was she thinking?"

"Well, to tell you the truth, I don't know. She's not one of my smartest wives. But she's cute. How about those tail feathers, eh?"

"I understand that a thoughtful human pedestrian dodged between the cars to aid her rescue and moved the bread slice off the road to get your little family to a safer place."

"Yes, I watched that. Very scary. I had a stern talk with her afterward. I'm grateful for the help, and I appreciate the chance to tell that to a human. You're the only one I know who I can communicate with."

"Well, that's very cool. I'll pass your thoughts along. That is, as soon as I figure out how to tell someone without sounding nuts. So Red, a couple more questions. How many wives and kids do you have and how do you keep track of them?"

"Gosh, well, I'm not good with numbers, as you might guess. Most chickens aren't. But I know that those hens and chicks by the museum and park are mostly mine. There's a bunch of skinny ones at Polihale and several really wet ones near Hanalei. They sneeze a lot. That's about all the family I can remember."

"Sounds like lots of step-chicks. You do get around."

"Yeah, kind of fun, actually."

"Well Red, I gotta go, been nice to chat. Where are you going now?"

"I'm going across the road. To get to another slice."

(Note: This story is based on a true incident. This happened when the then-editor of *The Garden Island,* Bill Buley, did in fact, retrieve a hen's food from the middle of the road near the newspaper's offices. Yes, the chicken was no doubt surprised (but alive) when her lunch and finally she and her chicks were all coaxed to cross to the "other side.")

Kaua'i Roosters Gain Altitude and Attitude

Last Wednesday five adventurous Kaua'i roosters convinced their "Rooster Whisperer" friend, Deputy Robert Moakane, to take them on a helicopter ride around the island. The deputy is known for his uncanny ability to mentally communicate with the local jungle fowl, much like a horse whisperer.

According to Moakane, the five had literally hen-pecked him until he agreed to pick them up in his patrol car and take them to Jack Harter Helicopters in Lihue.

"The Harter group was very accommodating—and certainly intrigued—so there was no charge, although I did bring them a couple dozen fresh donuts," quipped the Deputy. "There were the usual safety instructions and the birds had to agree to perch on old copies of *The Garden Island* newspaper just in case they had to, well you know."

This reporter smiled at that image and asked the deputy to continue.

"Well, they were noticeably excited, of course, as roosters don't fly all that well on their own," said Moakane. "About all the height they are used to is halfway up a kukui tree. So anyway, we all got settled in, the pilot winked at me, hit the throttle and the helicopter blasted off, zooming up and sideways at that awesome power-driven angle that only helicopters can soar to."

"Those startled birds were out of their seatbelts and all over the place in the back, fluttering and yakking and jabbering like a bunch of old hens," the whisperer continued. "They were all beaks and wings and flying-feathers-to-the-glass! It was a good thing the newspapers were there, especially when a couple of them threw up. You could tell that the other three were heckling the two motion-sickies, who appeared a bit embarrassed about it all. But, they perked up pretty quickly."

This reporter asked what area of the island most intrigued the fowl. The deputy thought that it was probably Mount Wai'ale'ale crater. "Then," he said, "I think Barking Sands Missile Range because, of course, they aren't allowed in there without a military pass. Also, we passed over an afternoon luau in Waimea and they seemed to snicker at the predicament that the imu pig was in, but shut up pretty quickly when we passed over one of the Chicken In A Barrel restaurants. Nevertheless, the ride was a wonderful excursion for them and certainly a first for me and Harter Helicopters."

When asked what may be next for the deputy and his flock, he replied, "Funny you should ask. When we passed over the cruise ship in Nawiliwili Harbor, they all quickly turned to me with their little eyes pleading and staring me down. I immediately said, Oh no, no way! No, not taking you on a cruise! Absolutely not gonna happen!"

He then added, "But, who knows! If I can get Captain Andy's or another to take us all on a trip like the Harter company did, well... could happen!"

Roosters Spotted Using Missing Laptops on Kaua'i

Unusually quiet roosters and hens and a dozen missing laptops were two mysteries solved in the morning on Kaua'i's North Shore. Both mysteries were found to be related.

"Roosters using laptops, well that's just ridiculous," said Deputy Robert Moakane. "But apparently, there is something to that."

According to the deputy's report, a dozen of the newest model laptops, which were originally suspected stolen a few days ago, had in fact probably fallen off a delivery truck. They ended up in a shallow ravine in Princeville. The computers were discovered to be scattered around a small area and were mostly face up, turned on and surrounded by dozens of very quiet roosters, hens and a few chicks.

"The whole scene was really quite odd," said island visitor Gavin Gardiner of Chevy Chase, Mich. "I couldn't believe how quiet it was yesterday morning. Normally, you know, those energetic roosters are crowing and yakking like all get-out. Instead, there was not a peep to be heard. It was so unusual that I got up and looked out my window early in the morning to see where all those pesky birds were. Come to find out, there were dozens of them right near my lanai, all gathered around these laptops. They had somehow gotten turned on and flock was literally surfing the web."

According to Gardiner, the younger birds appeared to be showing the older ones how to operate the computers. "In fact, one younger little guy seemed to be giving up on the older one as if to say, 'Oh just let me do it!' I could also see that one hen was on the Twitter site content to just sit on top of one of those 'new-user' egg images. It was all quite the scene.

"Another group of birds had the YouTube site up and were watching the trailer from Chicken Run," he said with a smile of delight. "They looked to be literally rolling around laughing and pointing, as much as chickens ever laugh and point.

"But what really struck me in the 'animal-imitating-humans' category was how most of the screen surfing was done by the younger chicks, while the older ones watched and apparently tried to learn," Gardiner said. "I could tell there was a lot of techy communication going on between the mid-age, or maybe 'teenage' chickens. They were just quiet and intent as anything and not paying a bit of attention to the older ones, who may well have been their parents."

As it turns out, a local concierge had ordered the laptops to be pre-loaded with island information to loan or rent out to guests.

After the computers were gathered up by the resort's staff, they were found to be in acceptable shape, except for one that an older rooster had given up on learning how to use. He simply left his opinion of the technology in a big blob on the keys.

"I actually watched that happen," Gardiner said, "and cheered him on! Personally, I think that is sometimes the appropriate response for these texting-surfing gadgets!"

Early-Morning Crime Results in Luncheon at Kentucky Fried Chicken

The Garden Island newspaper headline read "Defendant, witnesses, judge and victim's family invited to luncheon."

Very early yesterday, in a Princeville neighborhood, an assault resulted in the death of a young male. An island visitor was apprehended, brought to court later that morning and soon after released. Immediately upon release, the defendant, witnesses, the judge and relatives of the victim lunched together at a Lihue fast-food restaurant.

According to reports, the young male had been making an unusually loud and obnoxious "ruckus" of sorts in a Princeville neighborhood, near the 8th green of the Makai Golf Course, causing many of the residents to awaken sometime between 4:30 and 5:30 a.m.

Apparently, the disturbance consisted of "constant deafening noises and short, very loud outbursts," according to residents.

Even after having been "warned several times by the defendant," the young male continued to "aggressively, unabashedly and seemingly without remorse" continue his assault upon the peace and tranquility of the surroundings.

"The next thing I knew," said one witness, a dentist from Winnipeg wearing white and blue hibiscus pattern pajamas, "the sunburned defendant had the victim in his clutches and, well, shall we say, was able to end the commotion. Frankly, I was thinking of doing the same thing myself but he beat me to it. Well, since I was on my honeymoon, I didn't feel it was a good time to ruffle any feathers."

The perpetrator, caught red-handed and identified as Edwin Whitney of Aurora, Colo., immediately confessed to the incident and was treated to a cup of strong Kauaian coffee by a neighbor. Then he was immediately invited to a timeshare presentation, whenever he might be released from the police, and promised brunch at the Tiki Iniki restaurant upon completion of the one-hour—or more-likely-two-hour—timeshare presentation.

According to court records, the hearing was held at 11 a.m. in the Kaua'i County Courthouse, presided over by District Court Judge Judy Kahanamanahilohilomommamomm 'mahalo, who heard the testimony of the defendant, a few sleep-deprived witnesses—and a local chef whose commentary was described by a court visitor as "enthusiastically presented and 'spiced' with convincing words" that the annoying victim was "ready for killing and I applaud Mr.

Whitney for knowing." And then, apparently paraphrasing author John Grisham, "when it was 'a time to kill'."

It turns out that the judge was convinced by these testimonials that Mr. Whitney had reasonable motives to commit the very-early-morning act and soon acquitted the accused of all charges.

Immediately thereafter, the judge noted that it was, "nearing the noon hour" and suggested that all in attendance meet at the nearby KFC on Kuhio Highway for lunch.

She suggested that many of the victim's family were already in attendance and would not utter any objections. She also ordered that the victim, known to have been transported to court in an ice-packed Ziplok bag and marked as "People's Exhibit A," be given a proper burial "sometime after lunch." At that point it was noted that both the victim and the chef had quietly disappeared from the courtroom.

Rare 'Tofu Bird' Sighted Near Kaua'i's Haena State Park

Recently an island visitor confirmed the sighting of an elusive, mystical and—thought by many—to be mythical bird in the rain forest just south of Haena State Park on Kaua'i.

The fowl, which reportedly resembles a chubby male chicken and is more commonly known as the "Tofu Bird" by naturalist gourmands, was thought for years to be largely a fictional character created and promoted by certain Wall Street vegans who are heavily invested in pre-packaged vegetarian products.

Although rarely if ever sighted by ornithologists, especially without the use of binoculars or hallucinogenic tonics, the bird was thought to exist in various places such as near Haight-Ashbury in San Francisco, anywhere in Boulder County, Colorado and Kaua'i's North Shore, plus all of the continent known by geography professionals as Asia.

In fact, like Big Foot and the Loch Ness Monster, much has been written about possible sightings throughout history. It has even been given a Latin name by the discoverer, a pseudo-scientist from Ann Arbor, Mich. known only as Dude.

A self-described bird enthusiast and bird-feather collector, "Mr. Dude" had recently been seen chasing around the trails between Haena State Park and Hanakapi'ai Falls in hopes of adding the tail feathers of the Tofu Bird to his vast tail collection. "Yes, I've been chasing tail for many, many years," he admitted. He also officially affixed the Latin "Edamamae Vegane Fowl" name to the Tofu Bird Wikipedia website.

"Mr. Dude" more or less confirmed that this so-called Edamame, etc. bird, like most endangered and extinct species, tastes pretty good. "I was astounded, of course, when I finally sighted the rare bird and was able to get one good photo," he said. "I decided to pluck just one of the tail feathers as a specimen when I stumbled on some lava rock and accidentally stomped on the bird's neck. Gosh, it didn't move at all after that and I felt pretty bad. I was going to release it back into the rain forest but, well, I cooked it instead. I mean, what the heck! It was basically lifeless and I didn't know any veterinarians who could've fixed that mess. So I stopped at Big Save Grocery in Hanalei, picked up some olive oil and garlic, and took it back to the condo to cook 'er up!"

As suspected by many, but now confirmed by "Mr. Dude", the bird has neither skeletal bone structure nor any internal organs to speak of. "I personally am not into speaking of icky stuff like internal organs so I was happy when I didn't find any," he said. "Nope, except for the feathers, it was mostly comprised of tofu and makes a heckova good scramble. Although, I should have added some taro root. Darn, wish I had. Don't think I'm gonna get another chance like this one."

Asked by this reporter to present other scientific facts he may know regarding the mystical bird, "Mr. Dude" replied "Not much."

The question begs, did he have any other evidence besides the one photograph? "Other than the tail feather, which I seem to have misplaced at the moment, I have nothing much to show except a bit of indigestion because I'm pretty sure I used too much garlic. But I can confirm that it does, in fact, taste pretty much like chicken."

Kaua'i Roosters Rate Sports Illustrated Swimsuit Issue

No clue how the 2015 March Sports Illustrated magazine ended up as litter on Kaua'i's Ke'e Beach. Pages fluttering from the shoreline breezes under flapping palms, perhaps dropped by a careless sun worshiper, this was the Kaua'i-featured "swimsuit edition."

Kaua'i's natural curves in the photos' backgrounds were photographed mostly unfocused in contrast to the models', intriguingly more-focused curves, some perhaps more natural than others. This infamous issue was certainly tossed onto the right island.

The difference here was the number of roosters gathered around the pages. They were jostling for peeks and pecks at the pix!

Of course, that this not-quite-sports-oriented issue of the popular magazine was at Ke'e Beach wasn't the surprise so much as were the male jungle fowl queuing around it—that was the real show.

What's more, the roosters' hens were poised some yards away ostensibly chattering among themselves with disgusted, disgruntled stares darting back at the wanderlust males. The clearly stupor-induced fellows paid the ladies no heed, but instead studied the still-fluttering issue, peering back and forth with crowned heads bobbing from the photo pages to comrades-in-wings as though rating the images.

This reporter crept closer to photograph the literary group, assuming as always that they would scurry away, as roosters do whenever I attempt a personal chicken chat. My fowl communications are seldom successful and rarely result in anything more than rooster ramblings, which I generally translate to something like, "got any worms?"

However, this time they didn't scatter at all. The male flock held their beachhead, glancing up at me as though to ask, "Which one's your favorite?," with wings and beaks flipping colorful pages to-and-fro and then peeking up at me for a decision.

Realizing my chance to meaningfully converse with roosters, I pointed decisively to page 201. Featured there was a perfectly pleasant model posed in a Hawaiian-inspired bikini on the Polihale Beach with the southern end of the Na Pali coast presented as the fuzzy scene beyond.

My choice apparently took them by surprise. Huddling back together like a miniature football team, they debated with animated clucks and squawks as though arguing a bad call by the referee.

The boldest of the birds walked over to me, looked up and nodded a distinct "Yes, we agree!" I smiled, then checked the rest of the boy-flock to see nods of agreement. The male bonding was fascinating;

however, glancing to the ruffled hens I guessed the guys were having second thoughts about their magazine review.

Appearing to sense some unpleasant conflict, the big rooster rapidly chomped down on the magazine, dragged it over and offered me the offending issue.

After taking it away, I later revisited the scene to witness the old adage, "out of sight, out of mind". The guys and gals were back to their normal incessant hunting and pecking with no hint of fowl disorder. The big rooster looked up at me, cocked his head and seemed to say, "Got any worms?"

The World's Oldest Baby Chick or Is This a Stink about Nothing?

What is believed to be the oldest female jungle fowl ever discovered lives on the island of Kaua'i near Anahola and recently hatched what may be the world's oldest new-born baby chick, according to two local "odorologist" scientists.

Due to the advanced age of the mother, the chick was tagged as being approximately two months old at birth.

The mother hen has been observed for the past year by two scientists at the new Kaua'i Fowl Center (KFC) at Kaua'i Community College (KCC). This reporter asked the professors how they can tell the age of chickens on Kaua'i.

Dr. Burton Beagle explained that, "older birds smell differently than younger ones and both Dr. (Randy) Snuffles and myself are blessed with being able to smell better than most scientists. In fact,

I was voted as the strongest-smelling professor at Michigan State before I was encouraged to leave. That is, to leave and start KCC's new program."

The professors are attempting to document their theory that the age of chickens can be determined by their odor. Although this might sound preposterous in a sense (no smell pun intended), the odor research conducted by the two fowl-smelling scientists brought about the discovery of this particular hen.

"We knew that Kaua'i had an abundance of wild hens and roosters, so we aimed our advanced research here," stated Dr. Snuffles. "It turns out that of all the chickens on earth the Kaua'i birds are among the oldest, except those near a particular restaurant in Kapa'a. They don't live as long there, it seems, but that's a different research project that we generally take on around lunchtime," he said, while working a toothpick around his mouth.

"But, as for this one particular hen," Snuffles continued, "we found it on our first visit here and were able to track her scent and capture her to attach an ID band. She put up quite a stink, so to speak, but eventually we won out."

In an attempt to clarify an earlier statement by Beagle, I stated that I was confused as to how a chick, or anything for that matter, could be two months old at birth, versus being tagged as simply a newborn. The odor-absorbed scientists looked at each other before answering. "You know I hadn't thought about that, had you Dr. Snuffles?" asked Beagle.

"Well, no, not really, but the baby chick just smelled that old. Hmm…", came the reply.

Although this reporter found the discussion very interesting, it was obvious that this was not yet a complete news story. I announced that I would check back when their odor research more fully ripens. I left the interview with a profound urge to check the expiration date on the dozen eggs in my fridge.

Kaua'i Rooster on a Binge?

The rooster was drunk. Yes, had to be drunk. I'm very sure. The tell-tail signs were there. Smashed out of his mind, I'd guessed, but alive and randomly mobile.

Except for a crooked beak and crossed eyes, the mass of vibrant marmalade-orange and espresso-brown feathers was the majestic coat of a healthy bird. Husky, radiant, with his bopping head held high, elegantly regal. That is, when he wasn't throwing up. Dazed eyes, mischievous smirk or was it a gas-induced smile—hard to tell with a rooster—he was the stereotypical drunk.

Except, of course, he was indeed a rooster. He sported a confident but swaying head. A cocked head, of course. His self-assured strutting interrupted by random stumbling, his head up, then down to vomit, and back up as if to say, "Officer, I'm not drunk, no sirreeee..." Then he tripped, whacked into a nearby palm tree, squawked and tumbled inelegantly over—twitched a few times, then was quiet and still.

That's when my intrigue of observing the spectacle became, instead, concern. Did the head-whacking end his fowl life or was he just sleeping it off? Kaua'i jungle roosters are a hardy breed and there are thousands (Millions? Billions?) of them wandering noisily around this Hawaiian island, sharply alarming us humans about the advent of dawn. Each bird is colorfully unique. Tourists are intrigued by them and residents like them best when flattened by trucks and buried in unmarked graves. A love-hate sort of thing. Nevertheless, this exceptional rooster had my attention.

Not far from the now-dormant bird was a noni tree. And, of course under the tree was the infamous, notorious, misunderstood noni fruit that falls when ripe. This stinky, blue-cheesy fruit is known for its wonderfully nutritional and medicinal powers—if you can get it down past your taste buds.

I've tried it and can do that but am certainly amazed when birds devour it like it was peach cobbler! Imagine that! Well, here's the thing—noni fruit when it hits the ground, quickly ferments and bubbles to make a unique liquor-like substance ("alcohol"?) that I believe my soon-to-be-hungover rooster had been consuming like a cruise-ship visitor downing mai tais at a luau.

My curiosity got the best of me and I cautiously approached, close enough to witness his breathing and minor spasms. He was sleeping it off. Or maybe he was in a coma, which I would guess is pretty much the same when one has a brain the size of one of those tiny Ni'ihau shells.

I left him to his recovery but planned a visit in the morning to check whether he'd be back on wake-up duty and up-and-at-'em at dawn to dutifully make the required racket with his buddies.

He was not. But instead, he was leaning against a kukui tree with his head down and wings covering his ears (roosters must have ears, right?). He was nestled far away from the noni tree, appearing determined not to go there again. Maybe his brain isn't so small after all! Apparently it was just a rooster's version of "the morning after the night before."

Kaua'i Roosters and One Wild Turkey on Thanksgiving

"Tom! Come over here. In the bushes! We'll hide you."

"Thanks, guys," said Tom nervously. "They've been after me since Tuesday!"

"That's about the time we stopped crowing, just to be safe. It seems that those big predators sometimes don't know the difference between a turkey and a chicken," said Red, the leader of the Hanalei Rooster Regiment. "If we can make it past noon today without the chubby guys in the white hats and butcher knives finding us, we'll be safe for another year."

"But what is it with them especially wanting turkey," muttered Tom, "especially this one day in November. I want to be liked, of course, but not really in that way! Couldn't they just do with chick… oh, well, uh, chick peas, or poi, you know those tasteless things that even you roosters don't eat. And you guys eat anything!"

"Yep, it's true, we do eat anything and I know you're OK with gobbling, no pun intended, a bug or two."

"Yeah, but I don't crow about it!"

"Ha, ha, I get it. So, we've been talking and we think we can help you. Let's get moving. Trot on over here and we'll all hide in the bushes, behind Hanalei Surf."

"That should be safe from the hunters," Tom said, peering around, his head rotating like the beacon at Kilauea Point Lighthouse. "They'll all just head up the road or over to some food truck. I used to peck around the trucks after dark, but that stuff gives me gas."

"Yeah, the fries'll get ya."

"Say, Red, you got some good-lookin' chicks in your flock here."

"Ah, yes, we do, what are you…?"

"And, that brown speckled hen by the banana tree is a real looker, if you ask me. Hey, sweetie! Yeah, you! Wanna go look for centipedes on Saturday night?"

"Ah, Tom," Red said, with a questioning look. "You're a turkey, I don't think that…well, it's just…"

"Red, look, she's coming over to say hi! What's her name?"

"She's Hazel. But, umm Tom, she's sort of spoken for, like well, she's actually dating a rooster, not a turkey. Which seems good to me, actually. Really, Tom. *Really*?!"

"But Red, I hear that we live in an enlightened age. Hi Hazel, I'm Tom. You're a real pretty chicken. Love your beautiful orange eyes."

"Whoa, this is too much for me," interrupted Red. "So, I guess this is one special Thanksgiving for us, ya know, with you carrying on like this, with Hazel I mean."

"Why's that?"

"Well, this Thanksgiving we're more like the big folks. We're having dinner with a very, very fresh turkey!

Rooster Asks, "Why the Masks?"

"Mmmumberuffer haruph moffie corvid vackeen!"

"Red! What are you thinking?," exclaimed Kaua'i's renowned "Rooster Whisperer" Deputy Robert Moakane, staring raptly at his favorite rooster friend. "Red, I can't understand a thing you're thinking!"

The Kapa'a deputy has become well-known as Kaua'i's only accomplished communicator with the island's jungle fowl. And at this time, rooster Red, in an apparent state of confusion over the way the island's humans had recently changed their looks and language, sought the Deputy for an explanation.

The Deputy clarified to this reporter the way the "Rooster Whisperer-thing" works: "I talk to the rooster and then stare into his eyes to read his mind for responses. I know that sounds crazy, but I can do it. Unfortunately, Red does get distracted, so I don't want to relate everything he says, especially if there are some cute hens around. Let me relate the rest of this fowl/human conversation."

Red was questioning, "Deputy, why can't I understand what people are saying any more? I used to be pretty good at that."

"Well, Red, don't forget you're a rooster," reminded the Deputy.

"Yeah, like I'm gonna forget I'm a rooster."

"Well, I'm just sayin'…"

"But I used to understand most of the talking before you all started putting diapers on your faces."

"Ha! Diapers, I like that. How does a rooster know about diapers?"

"Babies, kids. I got dozens, hundreds of kids really, not bragging of course. But, you know, when I hear the big folks talk, I pick up stuff."

"Yes, and you mostly eat that stuff."

"Hey be nice! Don't knock it 'til you try it."

"No thanks, no worms for me."

"Hey, stop that, you're making my beak water! So, anyway, the only words I understand now are like, 'Where's my mask?' and 'Do I have to wear a mask?' And then the diapers go on and the rest is 'mmmumberuffer' or whatever. What's going on? Do you understand what you're saying to each other these days? And how come you're not wearing your diaper now?"

"Red, please call it a mask! It's not a diaper. But I'm not wearing one now because it's just you and me and yes, you're right sometimes our talk is a bit muffled with each other. So here's the thing. There's a big sickness called COVID going around and the idea is that if we wear our diapers, or ahh… I mean our masks, we won't give the sickness to each other. That's it."

"But you don't care if I catch this thing? What's up with that?"

"Red, I love the way you think but this seems to be special only for humans, not a problem for you chickens. But if you feel left out, I'll make you a mask and you can think things like 'mmumberuffer' if you like."

"No thanks, you humans make fun of us chickens enough already. If I wear a mask, the jokes are going to change to something like, 'the chicken crossed the road to get to the other mmmumberuffer.' No thanks!"

Unusual Early Gathering Sited at Anini Beach

The rumors sweeping through the North Shore of Kaua'i Sunday morning concerning an unusual wedding appear to be untrue.

According to initial reports, there was a large group of short, tuxedo-clad people gathered at low tide near the surf at Anini Beach. An eyewitness, a visitor from the mainland who asked that his name be withheld, gave his account to this reporter:

"I was up quite early yesterday morning after long flights from Michigan. You know how it is, that six-hour time difference and all. So when that first gosh-darned rooster started his thing, I couldn't sleep any longer and decided to get up and take a walk. I wished I'd had my binoculars with me, let alone my glasses, but I didn't. I'm a wee bit nearsighted.

"Well anyway, I was on the overlook by the Westin at about 5:00 a.m. and there looked to be 20 or so really short people—yes, all of them shall we say diminutive and every one of them dressed in tuxedos! They were just walking around slowly, kind of waddling around the water and beach. It looked like they were waiting for a preacher or something.

"Then it occurred to me, there were no ladies. These were all guys! I mean, I thought, this can't be a wedding. There were no dresses, just tuxedos! I thought, and then I thought again, and, ohhh! I immediately guessed that it was a wedding where there was no traditional bride, shall we say, and I put two and two together and well, that was that. I assumed they just chose the quiet early morning so that they wouldn't be disturbed by swimmers and snorkelers and so on.

"I thought it was pretty cool so I went back to the condo to get my glasses. It was about 6:00 a.m. at that point. When I got back to the overlook with my glasses, I realized my mistake. It wasn't a wedding of short men at all! It was a group of about 20 penguins that had gotten off a nearby iceberg to frolic on the beach.

"I said to myself, 'I've got to get a picture of this or nobody will believe it.' I went back to the condo to fetch my camera and by the time I arrived back to the overlook they had already scampered back onto the iceberg and were well on their way to floating off.

"I tried to take some pictures but my battery had just died. It was a real shame 'cause they seemed to be waving at me from way off with their little paws or fins or wings, whatever those things are. It was cute as all get out!"

This reporter then asked whether the observer had seen anyone else watching the event and he said, "I did talk to a couple of college-age guys who looked to be stumbling back from a heckuva party. I told them all about it and I pointed to the iceberg. They looked out toward the iceberg and saw all the waving and seemed to understand what went on. Of course, they were anxious to go tell their buddies, and I quote, 'if we could only find our car.' Unfortunately, I forgot to ask if they had a camera."

So there you have it—the eyewitness report of an event that at first appeared to be a highly unusual and inspired gathering for a formal wedding, and it turned out to just be penguins visiting the island.

Kaua'i Reporter Interviews Volcano Goddess Pele

The Hawaiian Islands' own Pele, goddess of volcanoes, fire, wind, lightning and mai tai hangovers, recently granted this reporter an interview at her residence, the Kilauea Volcano. The interview was conducted near the rim. From a warm, non-moving rock.

"Ms. Pele! Are you down there? Gosh, it's mighty warm around here."

"Aloha!"

"Ms. Pele, your Highness! Did you just say 'aloha'?

"Yes, aloha is everywhere. And you're from Michigan."

"Yes I am. How did you know that?"

"I'm a goddess. I know things. Not everything, mind you. I'm not like The Big Guy, but I've been around for a billion years."

"Amazing. So, may I ask how you learn things?"

"Well, we gods don't give away our secrets, but one way I learn is by listening to visitors who are scorching their Nikes on my rim. Tourists talk a lot. Not so much the guys, of course, but..."

"So, your Highness, do you only stay here or do you have other hot spots?"

"Ha! Hot spots! I get it. You're a funny guy. I like you."

"I'm kind of glad you like me."

"Why's that?"

"You could incinerate me."

"Yes, but I mostly gave that up after the Mount Vesuvius event. Never should have lost my temper there."

"Ah, so you get around. Are you part of all volcanic activity around the world?"

"Oh no, not all of it. The Vesuvius incident was during a Mediterranean trip with my cousin."

"Your cousin?"

"Yes, Cousin Thor. There we were. We got into it, arguing about who was stronger. He got all hot and blew up. I landed on my ash and blew out of town."

"Nasty. Do you have more cousins?"

"Yes, lots of cousins. Like Mahana. He created a few islands, like the one you call Easter Island. He was roaming around the Pacific, got sick and threw up. That's Easter Island.

"Threw up? Amazing."

"That's nothing. Cousin Vulcan was in Washington State a few decades ago and while napping at Mt. St. Helens, she accidentally sneezed. Not good. Tragic actually, but that's part of what makes up a volcano god. Lava happens."

"So tell me, Goddess Pele, tell me about Kaua'i?"

"Ahh, the good stuff. I'm glad you asked. That was my best work. A gorgeous place and nobody got hurt. Kaua'i is pretty cool, eh?"

"Yes it is, but surprising to hear you use the word 'cool'."

"Ha! I guess so. Well, I must get back to work. The Big Guy wants me to add a few hundred acres here and…"

"The Big Guy? You mentioned him before. Who's that?"

"Well, you know, The Big Kahuna? Our boss. Where the buck stops, that sort of thing. Actually, I can't say anymore. He likes to be mysterious and I could get into hot water. Ha! I said 'hot water'! I can be funny too. So, he's got a real-estate deal going and he claims he's going to need more land on this island.

"Real estate? That's strange."

"Not really. It's a timeshare thing. This is Hawaii. Need I say more?"

"Oh, guess not. Well, a real honor to talk with you. Mahalo for your time."

"Better move. I feel a sneeze coming on."

Too-Early Morning Joe

EERKK a EERRKK a ERRRRRK !

OK! I'm awake. Yikes, already. What's the ruckus? What's up!

It's 2:58 a.m.! 2:58! I am instantly reminded that roosters do not politely utter "Cock-a-doodle-doo" like in the storybooks, but in fact loudly shriek EERKK a EERRKK a ERRRRRK! Especially if at 3 in the morning. And repeatedly.

Not my time for a wake-up call! I assume my obnoxious, local rooster is beyond agitated. Why now? And he's loud LOUD! It seemed like he was in bed with me. Or he was way bigger than I had seen yesterday.

Stop it, I mutter, but muttering is not gonna stop it. All sorts of other, more lethal ways could stop it, but muttering is not one of them.

What happened to the 5:30 or 6 a.m. that he's known for? On a normal morning, I'm OK with him as my organic alarm. All good then.

But today! EARLY, LOUD AND RELENTLESS! Not the later, every-once-in-a-while crowing that comes with typical Kaua'i mornings.

Of course, I had no natural inclination to get up, but sleep wasn't an option with this racket under my window. This was too much. I had to know the cause of his incessant verbal eruptions.

With the lanai light shining, I was into an immediate stare-down with one ragged, wide-eyed, jittery mass of feathers. He was poised over some litter behind him, which I couldn't make out.

He looked up at me as though, "What do you want? Go back to bed!"—apparently finding his litter more interesting than looking at me.

Then, after another EERKK a EERRKK a ERRRRRK!, he lowered his vibrating beak and went back to intensely pecking away at his prey.

I wasn't aware that roosters had the munchies at 3 a.m. but this one surely did. He definitely wasn't shy about chumping on something, nor did he care that I was curious.

Inching up cautiously while he stayed the course, I then spotted his obsession. He finally stumbled away, in a coffee-jitters sort of way, to watch me inspect the goods.

Try to imagine what are the worst possible foods that a rooster can consume in the middle of the night? What could possibly make his early-morning SQUAWKING even earlier, more intense? More annoying? LOUDER? More 3 a.m. instead of 5 or 6?

It's coffee and donuts.

Yes, coffee and a chocolate donut, to be more specific. Well, a big chunk of a chocolate donut anyway. It was in a paper coffee cup, apparently soaked with just enough leftover java to make a chocolate-caffeine soup—a concoction abandoned near a "take-out" bag.

This boy had been going at the goodies, apparently as though a caffeine-and-sugar hit was his normal bird-brained thing to do!

EERKK a EERRKK A ERRRRK!

I was almost sorry to take away his 'drugs'—until he yelled at me again. Upon that, I figured that my sleep was more important than his addictions. Removing his buffet, I gently encouraged him to wander off into the jungle—hoping he would annoy the centipedes instead of me. The coffee-sugar crowing continued, but mercifully in a more distant, diminishing volume.

With ear plugs and two pillows over my head, it didn't take long to bring back my enjoyable sleep, dreaming of a quieter moment full of visions of my own coffee and chocolate donuts.

De-Roostering Our Island? Well, Not That Way!

Too many, I tell you! There's just too many!"

"What? What are you talking about?"

"How can the price of chicken keep going up at Safeway if I trip over those darned roosters in the parking lot!"

"Parker, you do know there's a difference between Safeway chickens and our jungle chickens, right?" board chair George Tyson asked.

"Well, I always wondered about that," Parker responded. "And speaking of chickens, do you think the smothered chicken at the food truck is from the jungle? And how do they smother it? With a little pillow?"

"Parker, you need a vacation. Maybe some nice quiet place, without so many chickens wandering around."

"But George, don't you think they're becoming a much bigger

problem? I really believe the chicken population on Kaua'i needs to be heavily curtailed. Or eaten. Don't you?"

"Sure, Parker, if you say so. Tell you what. Why not propose a solution to the board? I'm pretty sure you'll dream up something."

"I have an idea I've been thinking about. I'll discuss it with Dole and see what she thinks."

During the lunch break at the next Kaua'i County Board (KCB) meeting, Professor Maitai Dole, director of the KCB's new Tropical Organic & Farming Unusual Birds Program (TOFU), suggested to the group that to "get the jungle-fowl population under control, a live jungle rooster or hen could accompany every pineapple—and maybe coconut—that some tourists take home. You know, kind of a new pet. Now this isn't my idea. I need to cite board member Parker Panda for this concept. Thank you, Parker," she smiled, pointing her sandwich-filled hand toward Panda. "But I've given it a lot of thought and believe there is merit here."

She suggested that "perhaps the 4-H Club, Boy Scouts and other youth programs could build cheap cages from the island's bamboo so that the birds could survive the trip to the mainland.

"After the birds get on the airplanes, well, we don't really care what happens next, I would guess," the professor said. "That way we wouldn't do something so harsh such as just, well, you know, euthanizing them," said the professor, finishing the last bite of her Hawaiian chicken sandwich with extra pineapple.

"I think it's brilliant, if I do say so myself," offered Parker, who nodded to Chair Tyson and beamed a "pretty-smart-eh?" look. "Especially the bamboo part," he added.

After lunch, Dole offered the concept into a formal motion, which was rapidly seconded by Panda, the Kaua'i bamboo-plantation magnate. The motion passed unanimously.

That vote, however, was soon rescinded and a new motion with similar wording was tabled "for further study." The reason for this odd voting procedure was that, according to another board member, "It seemed like such a great idea at the moment, you know, because we're all tired of dealing with the increasing number of chickens, especially the obnoxious roosters. But then, after further discussion, we realized that we really hadn't considered the unanticipated consequences. You see, our pineapple chicken sandwich lunches are always so enjoyable, which really is why I accepted a position on the board, that we thought we should give this more consideration. I mean, this action could begin to raise the price of our lunch and, well, why would we want to do that?"

Avian
fresh
POP CORN
Kleenex
EGGS
Chick-O-Stick
HOW TO PREPARE CHICKEN DIVAN
By Henrietta
CHICK FLIX
EGGLESS
HOW TO
NO FOWL
How To
Your
They
CLEAN

Chicken Divan

(As told by Deputy Robert Moakane)

They were on the living-room couch. Most perched, some not. Some were undulating, babbling, wings-a-pointing, animated. Some were still, and mesmerized. A couple were asleep—on fluffy pillows. The whole scene was like halfway through the best-of-Friday-night college parties. Buddy-buddy comaraderie, as though they liked each other.

Fact is, chickens—roosters in particular—rarely party in groups, such as in "Hey guys, let's go check out the hens!" But there they were clustered, having the best of times, snacking away and jabbing wings like longtime pals.

Most appeared fascinated with the television, little beady eyes glued to the tube as if hypnotized. How the TV came to be on was a mystery—until I spoke with the owners the next day. They'd left it on to make it appear that the home was occupied. And, well, it was occupied all right! By roosters, hens and little chicks! Little chicks are the cutest—unless diaper-less on your couch.

The backstory: the day before, the neighbors had been curious about all the chickens gathered around that house. "We knew our neighbors were off island," said one observer, "and, of course, having a multitude of chickens scattered all over the place isn't unusual but there seemed to be an increasing number, a definite crowd, and they were chattering and energetically communicating, with nods and shakes. It just wasn't normal, in any sense of the word! It was definitely strange. I was afraid they may have gotten into the house and, well by golly, they had!"

One of the neighbors knew that I have a way with chickens—roosters mostly—and he contacted the police station, asking if the "Rooster Whispering Deputy" would do a chicken check. I said "sure" since the day was quiet right then in the policing world.

When I arrived, the chickens in the yard seemed to know I was not there to offer chicken feed and make nice. The flock backed away little by little, looking at each other as though I would 'cuff 'em and take them in. Of course, that would be a hoot, except not only were my handcuffs too big for their skinny legs, they would quickly peck their little beaks into me!

That's when I changed direction to peer through the front picture window. What I observed was my first clue that this would be a longer and more-interesting afternoon than just gazing at a bunch of yard birds.

There they were on the couch. A sight to remember. TV and popcorn—family time. A festive and exuberant crowd of chickens, earnestly watching the TV. Really? Could that be true? Well, as I looked further, it was true. It was quite the scene. A lively group of chickens, mostly on the sizeable vinyl couch.

And the surroundings were slightly messy, but not nasty. If popcorn hit the floor, it was immediately gobbled up, as were the Cheerios and other goodies, which they must have found in the kitchen. I couldn't take my eyes off the incredible scene but realized that I needed to put a stop to the merriment.

One problem being, of course, that they didn't know how to find the bathroom and probably—well not probably—wouldn't know how to use it. Therefore, well, let's just say, no matter that there was no popcorn on the floor, they did leave other stuff lying around, which would be a concern to anyone, especially the returning homeowner.

One younger rooster was intrigued with the TV remote, pecking away causing different channels to pop up, much to the irritation of one bird that grabbed the remote to remove it from the original pecker. A bit of a standoff ensued until some popcorn dropped from the couch and the first rooster, more intent on the food, abandoned the remote challenge.

It was time for me to act but I didn't know the best way. In trying to figure out how they had gotten in, I went around back and discovered a doggie door, slightly encrusted with colorful feathers. The evidence was discovered, and the mystery solved.

At that point, I reasoned that if I just barged in, they may panic and scatter all over the house, creating yet a bigger challenge. Instead, by gently tapping the window, I hoped to eventually gain their attention.

That seemed to be effective and little heads turned to discover me in the window. I waved. They didn't wave back. But there was a moment of stillness where everything stopped. I waved again. Looking around at each other, wide-eyed, they appeared to be quickly figuring out that "the gig is up." It was kind of sad now that I think about it. It's like that last day of summer vacation for kids. School—or in this case the jungle—awaits.

Roosters and hens scurried around and about, gathering up the chicks and then trotting off to the back door. They were lining up, haphazardly, to advance one-by-one through the doggie door.

One rooster, intent on taking the box of Cheerios that was clamped firmly in his beak, dragged it along until I rapped the window somewhat more soundly. His prize dropped as he scurried toward the exit.

I waited to enter until I believed they were all out, but then noticed one little check still under the couch, peering out as if to say, "Where'd everybody go?" The mommy hen turned and came back, searching around for her little one. Once found, she looked to scold the young'un to 'get a move on.'

The chick hastened out from under the couch, following mom to the doggie door. Taking one last look around, mom glanced up and offered me the evil eye—if hens can offer an evil eye!

Peering around the house corner, I witnessed the line of chickens silently trotting toward the jungle, back toward their usual stomping ground. That's when I knew it was OK to go inside and inspect their temporary roost. Having obtained the owners' entrance code, I did tidy up the place as best as a deputy is inclined to do.

Locking up and turning to leave, I glanced at the property's edge to see the flock watching my actions. That is, until they saw me place two large concrete blocks in front of the doggie door. With that they all turned around—heads down—to forlornly disperse off into the jungle.

The Author

Roger Lepley and his wife, Kristy, live in Kalamazoo, Michigan (Yes, there really is a Kalamazoo!) and have been frequent visitors to Kaua'i. They claim to know many of the chickens personally. Several of these stories have been published in *The Garden Island* newspaper, Roger's favorite island news source. The first story to be written and published was "Early Morning Crime Ends in Luncheon." It was written between the hours of 5 and 6 a.m. Yawn.

Roger is an architect and industrial designer, and Kristy is an artist and photographer. Thank you to past editors of *The Garden Island* who have published many of the submissions.

Thank you especially to our good friends, Fanny and Ron Bilodeau. Fanny is the renowned Kaua'i artist who personifies the island's chickens in oh-so-many clever ways. The image for the "Chicken Divan" story is an example. Roger's originally seeing her "chicken art" at the Kountry Kitchen Restaurant in Kapa'a inspired many of these stories.

www.ingramcontent.com/pod-product-compliance
Lightning Source LLC
LaVergne TN
LVHW021134160826
845679LV00016B/1740